Once there was a place called Bobville,
where everyone was named Bob. . . .

Welcome to
BOBVILLE
CITY OF BOBS

Written by ~~Jonah~~ Bob Winter
Illustrated by Bob Staake

schwartz & wade books · new york

In Bobville, where everyone was named Bob,
everyone looked exactly the same.

Of course, sometimes this made things confusing. When everyone looks exactly the same, how do you tell each other apart?

How do you even know who you are?

For the Bobs of Bobville, the answer was simple: You're Bob! Just like everyone else!

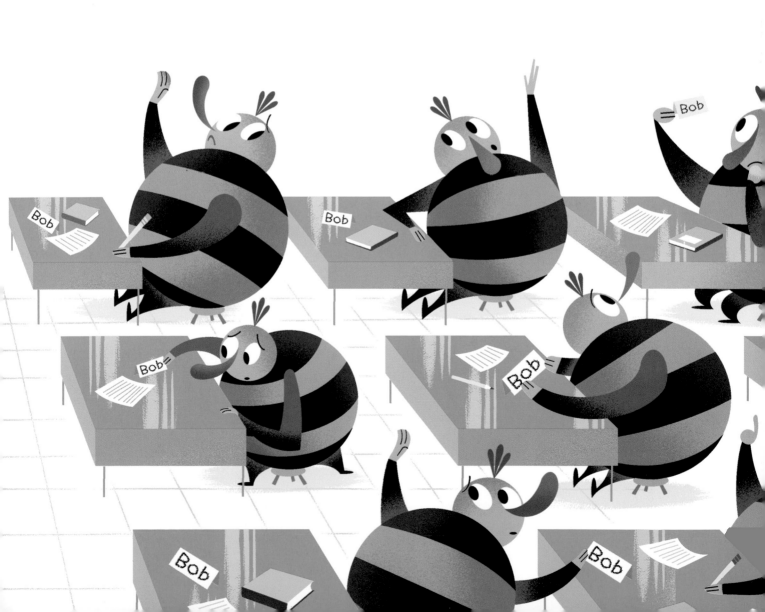

On the one hand, this was great, because—well, you never had to memorize anyone's name. You just knew it in advance!

On the other hand, life could get a little dull.

But mostly, these Bobs just loved *being
exactly the same*.
Every day, the Bobs of Bobville all got up
at exactly the same time.

They ate the same food.

They had the same hobbies.

They thought the same thoughts. If one Bob was thinking, *I'd rather be fishing*, you could bet your life that all the other Bobs were thinking that, too.

They listened to the
same music.

They went to the same movies.

They read the same books.

They even went to bed at exactly the same time—
and had the same dreams.

And they all agreed on everything, especially this:
They did not like anyone **not named Bob.**

They had heard on the news that such people existed.

People **not named Bob** had never been a problem, until one very interesting day. There was a certain Bob who woke up a little later than all the other Bobs, thinking:

I'm sick of the name Bob. I want to change it to . . .

And so he did.

He also thought:

I think I'll gel my hair today.
And so he did.

And: *I hate these clothes. I want new, colorful ones.*

And so he ordered some. He just felt like it, you know?

The next time he left the house, he looked different from all the Bobs of Bobville.

And of course, his name was now Bruce.

This did not go over well.

What kind of name is *Bruce?*

all the Bobs shouted.

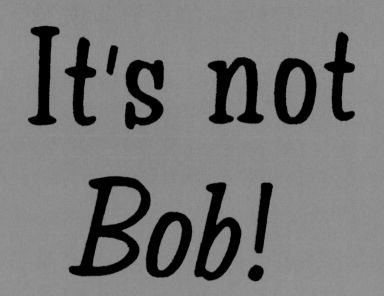

It's not Bob!

"And what's with those weird clothes?"

A town council was formed to discuss the matter.

It was decided that the Person Formerly Known as Bob

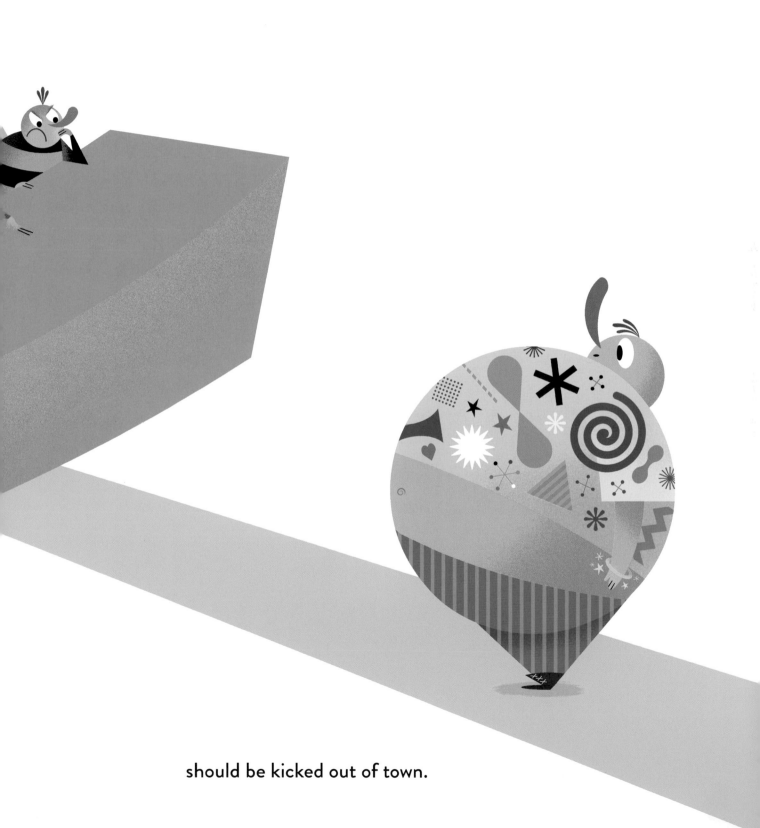

should be kicked out of town.

So Bruce was booted out of Bobville, while the Bobs got busy building a wall. After all, they needed to make sure this Bruise or Bryce or whatever he called himself couldn't get back in.

A wall would also be useful for keeping out other not-Bobs.

But guess what?

Turns out there was a big, exciting world outside of Bobville.
And while the Bobs of Bobville lived behind the huge wall
they'd built around themselves—

BOBS ONLY!

Bruce lived happily ever after.

For Little Buddy Bartrum —J.W.

To Dr. Pirundini, who gave us Bob 2.0 —B.S.

All rights reserved. Published in the United States by Schwartz & Wade Books,
an imprint of Random House Children's Books,
a division of Penguin Random House LLC, New York.
Schwartz & Wade Books and the colophon are trademarks of Penguin Random House LLC.

Visit us on the Web! rhcbooks.com
Educators and librarians, for a variety of teaching tools, visit us at RHTeachersLibrarians.com

Library of Congress Cataloging-in-Publication Data is available upon request.
ISBN 978-0-593-12272-3 (hc) • ISBN 978-0-593-12273-0 (lib. bdg.) • ISBN 978-0-593-12274-7 (ebook)

The text of this book is set in Brandon Grotesque.
The illustrations were rendered in pen, ink, and paint and compiled digitally in Adobe Photoshop 3.0.
Book design by Rachael Cole and Bob Staake

MANUFACTURED IN CHINA
2 4 6 8 10 9 7 5 3 1
First Edition
Random House Children's Books supports the First Amendment and celebrates the right to read.